# The
# SPOON OF DOOM

# The SPOON OF DOOM

Sam Hay

Illustrated by Hannah Shaw

**A & C Black • London**

*um*

First published 2010 by
A & C Black Publishers Ltd
36 Soho Square, London, W1D 3QY

www.acblack.com

Text copyright © 2010 Sam Hay
Illustrations copyright © 2010 Hannah Shaw

The rights of Sam Hay and Hannah Shaw to be
identified as the author and illustrator of this work respectively
have been asserted by them in accordance with the
Copyrights, Designs and Patents Act 1988.

ISBN: 978-1-4081-2399-7

A CIP catalogue for this book is available from the British Library.

This book is produced using paper that is made from wood grown in
managed, sustainable forests. It is natural, renewable and recyclable.
The logging and manufacturing processes conform to the
environmental regulations of the country of origin.

Printed and bound in Great Britain
by CPI Cox & Wyman, Reading RG1 8EX.

# Chapter One

I was halfway through my cheese-and-pickle roll when it happened.

'Yuk!' squealed Mandy Moon, who was sitting opposite me. 'There's something really horrible on your roll.'

I glanced down. She was right. It *was* horrible. Long, green and slimy. And just millimetres from my mouth.

'Don't worry,' I said cheerfully, 'It's only a marsh slug.' (As if that made it OK.)

Mandy wrinkled her nose. 'It looks disgusting.'

She was right (again). Marsh slugs *are* particularly unpleasant to look at. But as my dad will tell you (though you'll wish you'd never asked), they're not the slightest bit poisonous and actually taste quite nice. If you find yourself stuck in a marsh, there are worse things you could eat, because marsh slugs are full of useful protein and good for your gut...

See. I said you'd wish you never asked.

By now, Mandy was making a puking face, so I slid the roll (and slug) back into my lunch box and moved on to my crisps – less protein and not good for the gut, but far more my sort of thing.

I pretended nothing had happened. But Mandy was still in a state of shock. She was peering into my lunch box, watching the green slug slither slowly across the roll.

'Aren't you going to do something?' she said, unable to stop staring.

'Nope.' I was beginning to wish I could put Mandy in a lunch box, too.

'You're not going to take it home, are you?' she said, appalled.

It's the school rules, you see. What you don't eat, you take home.

'Yep,' I said, emptying the final few crisp crumbs into my mouth.

Mandy gasped. 'But what will your mum say?'

I shrugged. 'Something like "sorry about the slug, son, tomorrow I'll make sure you get a stink beetle instead".'

Mandy's mouth opened, but no words came out. So I snatched up my lunch box and scarpered. You see, sometimes I just can't be bothered explaining the weird world I live in.

My parents are entomologists. Or bug-botherers to you and me. Mum likes beetles and spiders. Dad prefers soft bellies – slugs, snails and worms. They met at bug camp when they were twelve and have been inseparable ever since. Love bugs – that's what Mum calls them. Personally, I prefer marsh slugs.

Anyway, they're totally besotted by mini-beasts. And our fridge is full of them. Hatching usually, which is all very well and interesting unless, like me, you prefer your butter without beetle larvae attached.

Personally, I am not the slightest bit interested in creepy crawlies. I never have been. When I was a small boy, I never worried worms. Nor did I collect spiders in small boxes. And to this day, I'm still perfectly happy for snails to go about doing their snail stuff without any involvement from me.

But unfortunately my parents have other ideas. They've even lumbered me with a buggy name. Albert Grub. Or A. Grub, as it says on all my schoolbooks. It's OK. You can laugh. I'm used to it. Sometimes I think I was adopted. What other explanation can there be for the fact that I have absolutely no interest in creepy crawlies?

My parents don't mind. They humour me. I, on the other hand, have to put up with living in their flea pit. Well, actually it's a house. But it's a total tip. There's dust everywhere. Bugs like dust. (I don't.) There are also strange experiments dotted around – like the old boot in the hall that has woodlice living in it. And the understairs cupboard that is strictly for spiders. (Mum says they're not poisonous, but I've seen them – they're purple for gawd's sake!) There's even an old scabby dog basket that's riddled with fleas. (And we don't even have a dog.)

Frankly, it's embarrassing. I don't dare bring any friends home – and certainly not since the incident with my best friend Barry.

He came round for tea a few months ago. Sausage and chips, it was, which was great, except Barry's dinner was already being enjoyed by a large cockroach that had somehow escaped onto his plate.

I was mortified.

And now, thanks to the marsh slug's appearance, I had to suffer the embarrassment at school as well. Enough was enough. As I walked home in the rain, I planned what I'd say to them:

*Grow up and stop playing with creepy crawlies…*

*Insects are not big and they're not clever…*

(Though that's not strictly true. Insects are exceedingly clever, as my parents constantly tell me. After all, there are a million trillion more of them than there are of us, and they've been around since the dinosaurs.)

But I didn't get a chance to tell my parents what I thought, because when I got home, I could see that something big and bad was afoot.

And somehow I knew it had nothing to do with the marsh slug that was sleeping soundly inside my school bag.

# Chapter Two

For starters, they were both there. Normally, when I get back from school, Mum is in her study working on her book. It's about beetles and she's been writing it for ten years. (What more can she find to say about them?) And Dad is in the garden tending to his gastropods (that's the bug-botherer name for slugs and snails – it makes them sound much more interesting than they are, trust me).

Today, they were also sitting at the table holding hands. Love bugs they might be. But they don't generally hold hands. Thank god.

On one side of the table was a stack of papers. Bills. Unpaid bills. I knew that because I'd sneaked a peek a few days ago and everything was written in red. On the other side of the table was a large and uneaten, slightly crooked carrot cake. Mum had been baking. That in itself was a bad sign. Mum only bakes when there's a crisis. So I knew something bad must have happened.

'Hello,' I said cautiously.

Mum turned to look at me. 'Oh, Albert,' she said with a slight quiver in her voice. 'I'm sorry…'

I grinned nervously. 'It can't be that bad.'

'Albert's right,' said Dad patting her hand. 'Something will turn up. It always does.'

'Not this time, Gordon,' said Mum, looking like she might blub. 'We've got a pile of bills. The roof is leaking. You've lost a marsh slug. And I've lost my job.'

I frowned. It had definitely not been a good day. (Though I reckoned I could probably solve the marsh slug problem.)

But Mum wasn't finished. 'So we'll have to cancel the holiday.'

I gasped. Now wait a minute … we'd been planning our holiday for months. Normally we don't do holidays. There's never much point. Mum and Dad only ever agree to go camping, and only to places that look like our back garden – muddy, marshy and full of slithery stuff for them to catch in jam jars. But this holiday was going to be different. I'd finally persuaded them to book a beach holiday. And I just couldn't wait.

I was about to start shouting when I saw Mum's

eyes fill up. I can't bear anyone blubbing, especially not Mum; it gives me the willies. So I quickly changed tack…

'Look, Dad,' I said cheerfully, 'I've got some good news.' I rummaged in my school bag and produced my lunch box. 'Your missing slug! Somehow it got mixed up with my cheese roll.'

Dad beamed. It doesn't take much to make him happy. But Mum just sighed. I realised the job thing had upset her a lot.

Mum stacked shelves at the local supermarket. But she said her head was too full of bugs to be much use to anyone most of the time.

'How did you lose your job anyway?' I asked.

She blushed. 'I fell out with the manager over a spider's web.'

That sounded about right.

'I just couldn't help it, Albert. There I was in amongst the baked beans when I spotted it. It was one of those special moments – you know…'

Nope. Never had one.

Mum looked dreamily at Dad, who gazed back sympathetically. 'No two webs are ever the same,' she continued. 'And this one was so magnificent, I just had to sketch it…'

I smiled as best I could. But inwardly I rolled my

eyes. My parents just don't live in the real world. My sympathies lay with the supermarket manager who wanted a shelf full of beans, not a wonderful spider's web for his customers to admire.

'Well, I've still got *my* job,' said Dad stoically.

Mum and I nodded. But we all knew the truth: Dad's part-time lecturing job at the local college paid peanuts. Small peanuts. Tincy wincy pip-sized peanuts that no monkey would swing twice for. We were definitely on our uppers.

Then suddenly I felt something land on my head. (Though that in itself wasn't unusual in our house.) Gingerly, I reached up to feel what it might be – an eight-legged arachnid. Or a six-legged beetle. Or something even more horrible. One of Dad's snails, maybe?

But no. It was water.

'I think we've got another leak,' I said glumly, as a second blob landed on the end of my upturned nose.

Mum finally burst into tears. And then it happened. Just as I was wondering whether I should stick down my lunch box to catch the drips, the doorbell rang, and life as we knew it changed for ever.

# Chapter Three

Actually, life very nearly *didn't* change for ever. Because I very nearly didn't let the bloke with the briefcase in.

'I'm looking for Timmy Piddler,' he said.

It sounded like a wind-up.

'You've got the wrong address,' I said crossly, about to close the door.

He looked at his notebook. 'Are you sure?'

'Yes. Absolutely. We're the Grubs,' I said. 'Which, I'm sure you'll agree, sounds absolutely nothing like Piddler.'

I'm not normally that rude, and certainly not to strangers. But I was too busy worrying about the future of my family to mind my manners.

The bloke peered at his paper again. 'This *is* 33 Cuthbert Close,' he said, looking past me into the hall. 'Perhaps I could speak to your mum or dad?'

'OK, but they'll tell you the same thing,' I said. Couldn't he see we were in the middle of a crisis?

Obviously not, because he stepped past me and found my parents, still holding hands, still blubbing.

'Dad,' I snapped. 'Tell this man there's no one called Timmy Piddler living here.'

But Dad didn't tell him. Instead he made a very strange face. His Adam's apple bobbed three times in quick succession. He gulped for air and then a shadow seemed to pass over him. His face went dark, and then pure white, and I thought for a moment he was about to have a heart attack, which really would have finished me off.

But he didn't. He looked at Mum, who had stopped blubbing, and then, in an 'I'm Spartacus' gesture, Dad stood up, shoulders back, shaggy head held high, and in a strange, deep commanding voice, he said, 'That's me. I'm Timmy Piddler.'

And then I felt *I* was having a heart attack. The blood began pumping very loudly in my ears. A thousand questions burbled up from my belly and got stuck in my throat, and I struggled to breathe.

*What*? What was he on about? His name was Gordon Grub.

And then suddenly I realised what he was doing. Dad was obviously so desperate to solve our family finances, he was about to break the law and commit identity theft. Whatever this bloke wanted with Timmy Piddler, Dad was ready to accept, good or bad.

It was quite brave, in the circumstances. After all, the bloke might have been about to steal our stereo to settle a debt. Or arrest him for some unpaid parking misdemeanour. Or punch him on the nose for some long-standing insult committed years ago by Mrs Piddler. Or, alternatively, and this was obviously what Dad was banking on, he could have been about to give him a suitcase full of lottery cash. Whatever it was, I couldn't let him do it.

'No, you're not!' I said firmly. 'You're Gordon Grub.'

But no one was listening to me. I was drowned out by the clicking open of the flicky clips on the stranger's briefcase.

'Excellent, then I have some rather good news for you, Mr Piddler,' he said.

# Chapter Four

Ten minutes later, Cyril Saltman of Saltman & Bone, Solicitors was sitting comfortably on our sofa, a cup of tea in one hand and a slice of carrot cake in the other. At his feet was his open briefcase (no cash, alas) and a bucket collecting drips from our leaky ceiling.

'So, just for the record, Mr Piddler,' he said, looking dubiously at the cake. 'When did you actually change your name to Grub?'

I leant forward. I wanted to know, too.

Dad looked sheepish. 'When I was 20,' he mumbled, scuffing the carpet with his slipper.

My brain suddenly started doing somersaults. Why had he changed it? Was he a spy on the run? Or witness to a really grisly murder – maybe a mafia hit or something. Maybe we were living under witness protection and his past had finally caught up with him and we'd have to move house and change names again. Maybe I'd finally get to say goodbye to Grub.

But no. Dad cleared his throat. 'I just fancied a change. I didn't really like being Timmy Piddler. Grub seemed to fit me better.'

*What?* Surely no one would *voluntarily* choose the name Grub. I had ten years of teasing as proof. What was wrong with Smith, or Jones, or Brown…

Dad grinned at me. 'I was a punk rocker back then, you know,' he said. 'As well as an entomology student, of course. Somehow Timmy Piddler just didn't work – not for a punk-rocking bug man.'

He had a point.

'Well, I have some rather good news, Mr Piddler,' said the solicitor. 'But first I must offer my sincere condolences to you and your family because I'm afraid I'm also the bearer of some rather bad news. Your great uncle Percival has passed away.'

The solicitor made a grim yet sympathetic face. One I reckoned he probably practised in front of the mirror.

Dad looked at his feet and shuffled uncomfortably.

'I do hope he didn't suffer,' said Mum gently.

'Oh no,' said the solicitor cheering up. 'He was 98, and passed away on holiday.'

If you had to go, that sounded like a good way to do it.

After a respectful pause, the solicitor started rummaging in his case. 'Now – to the matter of his estate…'

Suddenly, I felt a bubble of excitement. I know it was selfish of me. After all, we'd just heard that some poor old fella had passed away, but I couldn't help myself. You see we've never had much money. Nearly everything we own is second or third or fourth hand. And nothing works very well. The telly is older than Dad and my parents' idea of a games console is a travel scrabble set. Most of the time I don't mind, but sometimes, just sometimes, I long to be like everyone else.

The solicitor cleared his throat. 'I'm pleased to inform you that you are Mr Piddler's only living relative. And therefore his entire estate will pass to you.'

I gasped.

Mum gaped.

Dad looked at his feet again. Then suddenly he jerked his head up. 'Wait a minute,' he said desperately. 'I'm sure I have several aunts and uncles – and some cousins even. They must come before me – surely?'

I gave Dad a long hard look. I had the distinct feeling that there was something odd going on here.

It was as if he didn't want whatever it was that he was about to get, and he'd be pretty glad to offload it onto some unsuspecting relative somewhere.

'Alas, not any more,' said Mr Saltman. 'They're all sadly deceased. A series of unfortunate accidents means you are the last of the Piddler family.'

Dad looked decidedly uncomfortable.

Mr Saltman pulled out a pile of papers. 'I'm afraid there's no actual cash in the estate. And there's no residential property, either – your great uncle sold his house and furnishings years ago.' He scanned the paperwork. 'But there *is* his factory.'

*What?*

'He owned the Piddler's Porridge factory, and now it belongs to you.'

A tingle of excitement crackled through my bones.

But Dad wasn't smiling. 'I don't like porridge,' he said grimly. 'I've never liked porridge.'

I wasn't too keen on porridge, either, but that didn't stop me from dancing on the spot. We'd inherited a business. Maybe we were millionaires! Images of corporate jets and long limos fluttered into my brain. I pictured my parents swapping their scraggy jeans for nice suits and matching briefcases. No more slithery slimy stuff. No more embarrassing incidents at the dinner table when my friends came round. Hey, maybe we could even go on holiday!

I had a million billion questions bubbling inside my head, and as soon as Mr Saltman had gone (carrot cake wisely left untouched on the plate), I went on the attack...

*Why hadn't they told me we were really Piddlers?*
*Had Dad known about the factory?*
*And what was wrong with porridge anyway?*

But Dad just shrugged and sighed and then escaped to the garden to see to his snails.

Mum was unusually quiet, too, and after clearing away the cups, she bustled off to check on her ladybirds. (Three hundred of them currently live behind our bathroom mirror. Don't ask.)

So I was left to mull it over by myself. Why weren't my parents leaping around at our good fortune? After all, it isn't every day you inherit a factory.

It was a mystery. And my parents aren't generally mysterious people; they leave their letters lying around. (Always dull stuff about creepy crawlies.) They don't hide their bank books. (There's never much in the bank anyway.) And they always involve me in major decisions, stuff like: *shall we have fish fingers for tea tonight? Or baked beans on toast?*

Now, here we were, suddenly the owners of a secret cereal factory, and yet neither of them seemed the least bit excited at all.

# Chapter Five

Piddler's Porridge. The name rolled off the tongue nicely. But I'll admit it also left a bit of an aftertaste. It made me think of someone caught short at the breakfast table, and having to 'go' in their cereal bowl.

It was Saturday. The day after it all happened, and me and my parents were standing peering through the gates, gazing at Dad's inheritance.

The factory stood high on a hill above our town, in an industrial park where loads of old factories lay sprawled like dead dragons. Many were empty. Most were crumbling. And by far the crumbliest of all was Piddler's Porridge.

It was at this point I realised we probably weren't millionaires.

The factory was big and dark and ever so slightly scary looking. I think it might have originally been red brick. But now it was soot black. A high wall surrounded it, with an ancient old metal gate at the front. There were no lights on. And the only evidence that something might actually be happening inside was a finger of pale smoke that rose from the chimney.

This wasn't quite what I'd imagined. But I tried not to show my disappointment because Dad wasn't looking happy, either.

He sighed deeply. 'I suppose we'd better show our faces.'

'Try not to worry, Gordon,' said Mum, taking his hand. 'I know it'll be all right.'

But Dad didn't smile. His fists were clenched. And he was grinding his teeth.

I should explain at this point that my dad's not normally so sulky. He hasn't got a temper. And he never shouts. I know there are dads like that. I've seen them at school concerts. They're the ones who look like someone's superglued their feet to the floor to prevent them legging it.

My dad's a bit like a clever collie – generally amazed by the world, and interested in everything. He's tall and skinny with shaggy hair, and he often forgets to shave so he looks a bit of a scruff. He wears baggy cords and holey jumpers, not because he doesn't have a few nice ones, but because he prefers stuff that's been 'worn in', as he puts it.

Mum adores him, which is odd. Because if I was a girl, I'm not sure he'd be adorable. His nails are dirty and his hands are always covered in slug slime. He can't dance. He can't cook. And when he's not out bothering bugs he likes to play guitar very badly. But he does smile a lot. So maybe that's something.

Today he wasn't smiling. He was glowering. Thankfully, it was not for long…

'Timmy?' said a gravely voice. 'Is that really you?'

I'd been so busy peering at my dad, I hadn't noticed the small, round-faced bloke who'd suddenly appeared on the other side of the gate.

'Ernie!' gasped Dad, a grin exploding onto his face. 'I didn't know you were still here.'

Ernie beamed back. And, after a brief fumbling of keys, the gate squeaked open and the two men embraced warmly.

'Look how you've grown,' said the old bloke, looking up into my dad's shaggy face.

'Well, I am 45,' mumbled Dad shyly.

'Blimey,' said the man. 'That means I must be 309.'

They both laughed. And then Dad remembered me and Mum.

'Ernie, this is my wife, Lottie, and my lad, Albert.'

Ernie grinned at Mum, and then turned to me. He swept up my hand in a manly shake, and for a moment I thought he'd crush it to dust, because his forearms were like elephants' thighs. (A consequence of a lifetime of porridge pounding, as Ernie later explained.)

'Welcome to Piddler's, lad,' he said, delightedly. 'I'm Ernie Moon, the foreman.'

His face actually looked like a moon, or perhaps more like a big bowl of porridge: cream-coloured and slightly lumpy. For a second I had a sudden panic that my face might become like that if I spent too much time at Piddler's.

Ernie winked at me. 'So, Albert, are you ready to taste the wonderful world of porridge?' He grinned mischievously.

I nodded.

'Then follow me!'

And we were off, down the concrete path and heading for the huge wooden doors at the front of the factory.

I'm not sure what I expected to see. But it wasn't what we found. Through the doors, a small lady was sitting behind an enormous empty desk, and she was knitting.

'This is Margery, our receptionist.'

The lady smiled. But didn't stop knitting.

Past Margery, we followed Ernie down a long, dark corridor, then up three flights of stairs and down several more dusty old corridors.

Everything looked ancient and broken (a bit like our house); there were giant holes clawed out of the walls, as though someone had started DIY and then given up. It was also a haven for bugs. Woodlice clung to the stairs. Beetles scuttled in the dirt. And cobwebs wound themselves around the banisters and light fittings. (Needless to say Mum's eyes were like pies.)

Eventually, we came to a big brown door.

'This was your uncle Percy's office,' said Ernie. 'I thought you might like to see it again, Timmy.'

Dad mumbled something I couldn't quite hear, and Ernie just smiled a sad sort of a smile. Then he unlocked the door and heaved it open.

Mum gasped. I jumped. And even Dad swallowed hard. Because there, standing staring at us in all his old-boned glory, was Percival Piddler himself.

# Chapter Six

Of course it wasn't *actually* him. After all, he'd been dead for some time. Can you imagine the smell?

No. Probably best not to.

It was his *portrait*. A life-sized picture of the man, taking up almost an entire wall of his office. Actually, he looked just like my dad – a well-ironed ancient version of Dad – as though Dad had finally grown out of bugs, had a decent haircut and taken up carpet bowls. Not that any of those things seemed to have made 'Dad' happy, because the man's expression was exceedingly stern.

It was quite unnerving, as though the old boy was watching us, judging us, and quickly deciding we weren't up to the job of running his business. I quite expected him to step off the wall and shoo us all out of the factory.

But of course he didn't.

Dad frowned. 'Did Uncle Percy still come to work each day? I mean, right up until the end...'

'Never missed a day,' said Ernie grimly. 'Until he decided to go on that final holiday – mountain climbing in the Alps, it was. A strange choice for a man of his age … and then when we heard he'd fallen off a mountain and broken his neck. Well, it was a shock to say the least.'

I gulped. I'd never met anyone who was dead before. I stared up at the scary old portrait and Uncle Percy's eyes seemed to stare right back at me. I shivered and moved closer to Dad.

Ernie sighed. 'Until he died, he practically lived here at Piddler's. That was his bed over there.'

Sure enough, under the window was a rather uncomfortable-looking camp bed, still made up with corrugated-iron sheets.

'But why?' I gasped. 'Why would anyone want to sleep in their office? Was he too poor to have a house?'

Ernie shook his head and smiled sadly. 'No, lad, though you're right in some ways. The business has fallen on very hard times. Half the factory is empty now. We don't make as much porridge as we used to. But that's not why your great uncle Percy slept here. He was a driven man. He was searching for something…'

I wanted to ask *what*, but Dad coughed and asked

Ernie to show us the rest of the factory.

I noticed Dad's smile was missing again. And it wasn't the only thing. Mum had also disappeared. But there was no time to mention it, because Ernie was off – leading us out of the office, down the corridor, across a landing, and down more stairs. And then suddenly I heard a distant rumble of thunder from beneath my feet.

Ernie grinned. 'Old Bertha's awake.'

What?

'The generator, Albert,' said Dad managing a slight smile. 'It powers the factory. She's known by everyone as Old Bertha.'

I eyed Dad suspiciously. He'd obviously hung out at Piddler's a lot – so why hadn't he told me anything about it?

'Now then, Albert,' said Ernie. 'Through here is the changing room. We'll get you kitted up, and then you can come and see what we actually do.'

I was bundled into overalls, a hairnet, white wellies and a ridiculous-looking hat. Thank God no one from school could see me. Dad looked even dafter than me, but I didn't get a chance to tell him because now Ernie had heaved open another big door and suddenly I found myself being suffocated to death by the pungent perfume of porridge.

30

It stinks. Honestly, it does. When you get up close and personal with an enormous pot of porridge, the smell knocks your spots off. For a few seconds I thought I might keel over and have to be carried out by a gang of porridge workers. But gradually my lungs started working again, and my nose began to acclimatise. I noticed Ernie and my dad breathing deeply; gulping in large gobfulls of the stuff.

I looked around. The factory was weird. I've seen plenty of those 'through the round window' sort of kids' telly programmes – where they show you how they put the goo inside a cream egg, or get the bristles onto a toothbrush. There's always loads of machinery involved. Not here. Though there *was* a conveyor belt. Hundreds of shiny tins were merrily bobbing their way along it, now approaching what I reckoned must be called the 'big blobber', because every second or so it would squirt a big blob of grey gunk into each tin.

Directly above the big blobber was a platform with a giant metal cauldron in the middle, where two enormous workers stood stirring the contents mechanically.

And that was it. That was the extent of the industrial revolution as experienced by staff at Piddler's.

Actually, I'm fibbing. There was one final process. Once the blobbed tins reached the end of the conveyor belt, a large metal hammer thing bashed each one on the head, hammering on a lid I supposed. Then a big bloke with even bigger arms than Ernie, gathered up the tins and carried them to a table where more workers sat, sticking labels on them.

It was like something out of the Dark Ages. Where were the mechanical robots that could stick on a hundred labels a second? Where were the huge industrial ovens mixing up the food, controlling the temperature, and making sure every tin was exactly the same? And, hey, since when did anyone eat porridge from a tin anyway?

This last point I put to Ernie, though I had to shout it out over the din of the clanking tins.

Ernie grinned. 'It's actually quite popular,' he yelled back. 'We have customers all over the world.'

I was shocked. There was a whole global community of tinned-porridge guzzlers that I knew nothing about.

'We make three types of porridge,' yelled Ernie enthusiastically. He reached into a pallet and produced a tin.

*Piddler's Pride,* I read.

'That's our bog-standard brand,' shouted Ernie. 'It does what it says on the tin.'

Fair enough.

He selected another. 'This one's more special. It's our luxury brand.'

*Piddler's Premium Porridge – thick and creamy.*

'Fit for a king, that is,' he shouted, winking at me.

I smiled politely. (It was almost as bonkers as the world of bugs.)

'And this is my favourite,' he boomed, selecting another.

*Piddler's Prune Porridge.*

Prunes. And Porridge. I suddenly felt slightly queasy.

'Look!' yelled Ernie. 'They're switching to prune now…'

I watched as yet another gang of enormous porridge workers heaved a new cauldron up onto the gantry above the big blobber. And suddenly the bobbing tins were being filled with purple goo instead of grey.

It was mad – handmade tinned porridge – the factory was truly loopy. But I liked it. Honestly. I did.

# Chapter Seven

I've no idea why, but as we left the porridge room I couldn't stop smiling. Secretly, I'd quite like to have snuck back inside and stirred the porridge myself a few times, or even stuck on a few labels. I imagined myself growing arms like tree trunks and developing a taste for premium brands of Piddler's.

The smell had obviously got to me; addled my brain, or something. Because before today, I'd always thought porridge was about as exciting as a pair of beige trousers. Not now. Suddenly it seemed … well … sort of cool.

As I took off my overalls, I peered down at my wrists and wondered whether it was my Piddler blood that was making me feel this way. Whatever it was, I felt a bubble of excitement in my belly. Perhaps that was Dad's trouble, too. Because he was strangely silent. Even Ernie didn't say much as he led us back to reception.

And then suddenly it came out: 'So, Timmy,

what do you say? Are you going to stick around and see us through?'

Dad shuffled his feet and tugged on his tie. (Bug men don't generally wear ties.)

'Well, I'm not sure, Ernie. I mean, it's great here and you guys do a brilliant job, of course...' He swallowed nervously a few times, and tugged at his tie some more. 'But as you probably remember, I'm not really keen on porridge, or business, and I think it would be better if we were to sell the firm to someone more ... capable.'

*What?* What was he on about? How could Dad sell the factory? We'd only owned it five minutes.

I was about to shout when suddenly the front doors burst open and a small group of smartly dressed people appeared. The bloke at the front spotted Dad and made a beeline straight for us, totally ignoring Margery the receptionist.

'Ahhh! The Grubs, I presume,' said the man, a towering beanpole. He beamed broadly and stabbed a pin-thin arm at Dad.

As they shook hands, I noticed Ernie gave him a serious scowl. And for some reason I felt like giving him one, too.

'My name's Snoodle – Smedley Snoodle from Snoodle's Noodles.'

It sounded like a riddle.

I wanted to reply, I'm Albert Grub, rub-a-dub-dub. But somehow I didn't think he'd laugh. And anyway, he wasn't the slightest bit interested in me.

'I'm your neighbour,' said Smedley, clapping my dad on the back and smiling like a crocodile. 'My noodle factory is next door.'

Dad smiled. But Ernie didn't. I could see the hairs on his enormous arms bristling crossly. And then suddenly a small klaxon went off inside my brain.

Snoodle's Noodles. SNOODLE'S NOODLES? They were the finest instant noodles in the world!

I loved them. All five flavours – *Turkey Dinner*, *Onion Bhaji*, *Steak and Kidney Pie*, *Chicken and Chips* and, my personal favourite, *Kebab 'n' Ketchup*. They were great. You stuck them in the microwave and they were ready in seconds. My sort of food. And here, standing in front of me, was the man who made them. I was speechless. I wanted to blurt out how much I enjoyed his noodles, but he was too busy grilling Dad to notice my excitement.

'I heard from old Piddler's solicitor that you were coming here today,' said Smedley, looking around disdainfully. 'Awful, isn't it? I mean, they try hard, but they're living in the past.'

Ernie's eyes narrowed.

Smedley looked closely at my dad. 'If you don't mind me saying, Grub, you're not a porridge man, are you?'

No one could argue with that.

'And I'd also say – forgive me if I'm wrong – that you're not actually a business bod, either.'

Dad shook his head sheepishly.

'Don't worry, Grub,' said Smedley with an insincere grin. 'I have a solution that'll suit us both – sell Piddler's to me.'

I was gobsmacked. Ernie growled. Dad started to look slightly sweaty.

Smedley held up his hands. 'Yes, I know it's out of the blue – a surprise, a shock – but that's just the sort of chap I am. Instant ideas. Instant decisions. Instant noodles. After all, why wait when you know what you want?'

Ernie could stand it no longer. 'Get lost, Snoodle,' he said, stepping forward at last. 'Everyone knows you're not interested in Piddler's.'

Snoodle glared back at the old foreman. But I noticed him retreat slightly. Ernie might have been older and smaller than him, but one flick of his forearms would have sent that skinny spider spinning.

Snoodle turned back to Dad. 'I'll give you a fair price, Grub. Trust me.'

'Don't do it, Timmy,' said Ernie desperately. 'He doesn't care about Piddler's. He'll close us down – sack us all. He's just after the spoon.'

*Spoon?* What spoon?

'Mr Grub knows what's best for his family,' said Smedley Snoodle, starting to look cross. 'And this crumbly old factory isn't it.'

But Ernie wasn't giving up. 'Think about it, Timmy. You mustn't let him get it. You know what happened the last time that spoon fell into the wrong hands…'

What spoon? Why did Ernie keep talking about a spoon? I looked at Dad. His Adam's apple was bobbing wildly. And his hair was standing up on end. He tugged at his tie, and this time he tugged it right off.

And then he shook his head sadly. 'He's right, Ernie – I'm just not the man for the job. I'm sorry…'

And then I realised what he was about to do.

'Dad,' I said desperately. 'Don't do it. Don't sell Piddler's.'

But I needn't have bothered, because just at that moment…

'GORDON! GORDON!'

It was Mum, pounding down the corridor, her face bright red, her eyes wide like saucers.

'Gordon, you'll never believe this. Guess what's living on the roof of the factory?'

If she'd said the Loch Ness Monster, I wouldn't have batted an eyelid.

'Jumping spiders!' she gasped.

And we all sort of sagged. All, that is, apart from Dad.

# Chapter Eight

Mum often does this sort of thing. Just when the world looks like it might be about to crumble, she suddenly appears and somehow manages to avert Armageddon. She should work for the UN really.

She gave me a wink, and I wondered how much she'd heard before making her grand entrance.

'And it's not just spiders, Gordon,' gasped Mum breathlessly, 'there are some amazing worms outside in the factory garden. It's fabulous here – you must come and see.'

Dad grinned gratefully, like a drowning man thrown a life raft, and without another word, he took her hand and escaped.

I was left with Ernie and the Noodle crew.

Smedley Snoodle muttered something under his breath, and then withdrew to huddle near the door with his gang.

'What was all that about?' I whispered to Ernie, who was exchanging knowing looks with Margery, still busily knitting behind her desk.

He shrugged apologetically. 'You'll have to ask your dad, Albert. It's Piddler family business.'

But I wasn't about to be fobbed off.

'Why does Mr Snoodle want to buy Piddler's? You said he wasn't interested in porridge.'

Ernie looked slightly uncomfortable and then shrugged. 'I shouldn't think he is – why would he be? But there's obviously something in this factory that he wants.'

'You said something about a spoon. What spoon? Come on! You've got to tell me. Dad won't. I didn't even know we were called Piddler until last night, let alone anything about the factory.'

Ernie sighed. And I could see he was weakening, so I carried on.

'I don't want him to sell your factory. Not now. Not ever.'

And I meant that – every word. You see, for some reason Piddler's felt like a good place to be, and I wanted to be part of it. More than that, I wanted my parents to be part of it. I wanted them to stop playing with bugs, and work at Piddler's instead. Maybe then I could put my slippers on without having to check whether something slimy had got there first. And I could kick a ball round the garden without endangering Dad's worm world. (We don't have a compost heap – we have a compost continent, with thousands of the blighters inside.)

There must have been something desperate in my eyes because Ernie suddenly took pity on me.

'Come on, lad, let's get a cuppa and I'll tell you a bit – but your dad won't like it.'

As he led me away, I tried not to look at the Noodle crew, still huddled by the doorway. But I could feel their eyes boring into my back.

We went to the staff canteen. Ernie said the shift was changing because one minute it was empty, the next it was full of moon-faced folk with thundering forearms and cheery smiles. Porridgers. That's what Ernie called the workforce. And a strange-looking bunch they were, too.

Ernie got the tea (though I have to say it tasted like porridge), and sat me down at the back of the room, and then slowly, a bit like porridge coming to the boil, he told me the tale – all about my dad, Piddler's Porridge and, most importantly, the spoon.

'Your dad was orphaned as a baby,' said Ernie. 'Sad, it's true, but I suppose it was better that he didn't know his parents; after all, you don't miss what you don't know.'

**43**

I felt a lump in my throat. I'd never really noticed I didn't have grandparents on Dad's side. He never mentioned his family, and I never asked.

'Your great uncle Percival took him in. He was a good man back then; full of ideas and energy. Business was booming and he was grooming your dad to take over the factory, but of course your dad had other ideas…'

'Bugs?' I guessed.

Ernie smiled. 'Percy thought your dad would grow out of them…'

Fat chance.

'…then the bottom fell out of the tinned porridge market,' sighed Ernie. 'And Piddler's was in trouble. There was even talk of closing down the factory. Your uncle had to lay off half the workforce. They were terrible times.' Ernie shook his head sadly. 'But there was worse to come. Around then, your uncle found one of your dad's old picture books. A fairy story – *The Magic Porridge Pot*. Do you know it?'

Of course I did. Every kid did – a little old lady gives a girl a magic porridge pot, which eventually goes haywire and floods a village with porridge.

'But what's that got to do with Piddler's?' I asked impatiently.

Ernie looked embarrassed. 'Your uncle became obsessed with that story. 'Imagine,' he'd say, 'a pot that produces endless porridge with no ingredients, none at all. If only we had that pot, we'd be billionaires…"

'But it's just a story for little kids,' I said.

'Of course it is. But as I've learnt to my cost, Albert, in every fairy story there's just a grain, or perhaps in this case a tiny *oat*, of truth.'

I didn't believe a word.

'Anyway,' said Ernie, 'your uncle started looking into it. He read every book he could find. He

**45**

consulted historians. He even went to the British Museum – they thought he was barmy. And then, finally, he hired a man to travel the world and search out the truth of the tale.'

'But that's bonkers,' I said.

'You're right,' said Ernie, taking a slug of tea. 'But I never said your great uncle Percy was sane… The smell of porridge gets to you after a while – we're all a bit doo-lally at Piddler's.'

Maybe *that's* why I'd suddenly developed an interest in porridge. The smell had got to me. It had certainly got to Ernie. What a yarn he was spinning! 'Then one day the man returned from his travels with a strange story.' Ernie lowered his voice. 'He said he'd found a village in Russia that had actually been flooded by porridge, just like in the book. High in the mountains, it was, in a big swampy gully – a sunken village where the roofs of the houses, submerged below, could still be seen from above.'

For no reason at all, I suddenly felt slightly cold. I hugged my porridgy tea closer.

Ernie took another slug of his and paused for a second. 'According to legend, the villagers bought a magic spoon from a pedlar. He'd promised them that if they used it to stir their porridge pots, it would make more and more porridge. It was a godsend for a hungry village in the grip of winter. But then one day it went wrong. And it carried on making porridge until the whole village sank.'

I grinned. 'You're pulling my leg now, and anyway this was supposed to be a story about a magic porridge *pot*...'

'Not a pot, Albert. A *spoon* – the Spoon of Doom, they called it.' Ernie's eyes darkened and his voice dropped to a breathy whisper. 'Everyone in that village died, Albert – drowned in porridge. And I'll tell you something else, lad, our own town very nearly suffered the same fate.'

I gasped. 'How?'

'Because Percy's man brought back that spoon with him. And he gave it to your uncle. Percival Piddler got his hands on the Spoon of Doom.'

# Chapter Nine

I felt like laughing. 'But that's ridiculous,' I said. 'If that village *really* existed, and it *really* was flooded by porridge, then the spoon would have been lost for ever.'

'It was, lad. It had been lost in that swamp for hundreds of years, and that's where it should have stayed, but unfortunately your uncle's man hired a diver to find it.'

I shook my head. 'But he could have found any old spoon. How did he know he'd found the Spoon of Doom?'

'Because it was the only thing left in that sunken village that wasn't cracked or crumbling or rusted or rotten. Piles of skulls and bones and one perfect wooden spoon, that's all the diver found.'

I still wasn't convinced. And I was beginning to think Ernie was as doo-lally as Uncle Percy.

'So what did Uncle Percy do with it?'

'He used it, of course. The very next day he

gathered us all together in the porridge room –
your dad, too – and we watched him climb onto
the gantry and start stirring the porridge pot with
that big old spoon.'

I tried to picture the scene.

'At first nothing happened. And I'll admit,
Albert, I laughed to myself at your uncle's folly…
Everything was working normally, you see. The
porridge cooked, and when it was ready, it started
squirting through the funnel into the cans below,
just like it does now. Then, after a while, the
porridge pot should have run dry. But it didn't.
It kept on squirting out porridge – hundreds and
hundreds of tins of the stuff. And still it made more.'

I took another sip of tea. It definitely tasted like
porridge.

'Soon we ran out of tins, so we filled tubs, buckets
– anything we could find – but we couldn't keep
up and the porridge started spilling onto the floor.'
Ernie shook his head. 'And then a really strange
thing happened - your uncle stepped away from
the pot and the spoon carried on stirring all by
itself.'

'But that's impossible!'

Ernie shrugged. 'Your uncle was mesmerised.
So was your dad. He'd climbed up onto the gantry

to get a better look and was horrified at what he saw. The spoon was turning faster and faster, round and round like a twister, and the faster it spun, the more porridge it made. And then I realised there was a real danger that the factory would flood. 'Everyone out!' I shouted – and the porridgers ran for their lives.'

'What did you do?' I gasped, completely caught up in the story now.

'There was nothing I could do, lad, because at that point I felt my feet stick. The porridge wrapped around my legs and tried to suck me under, like quicksand. I shouted to your uncle to stop the spoon, but I don't think he could, even if he'd wanted to.'

'So what happened?'

'Well, the porridge was up to my armpits. It was all I could do to stop myself from sinking. I was clinging onto a pallet, and more and more porridge was pumping out.

And then your dad did the bravest thing I've ever seen. Just when I thought I was going to drown, he reached into that cauldron and pulled out the spoon with his bare hands.'

'But wasn't it hot?' I gasped.

'Burning hot, lad. But it did the trick. Your dad broke the spell. He got the spoon out and suddenly the porridge stopped flowing.'

Ernie looked worn out. He sighed deeply and drained the last of his tea. 'You should have seen the factory, Albert. What a mess. It took weeks to clean up.'

'But what about Dad? Was he OK?'

'He had burns up both arms, poor lad. But that didn't stop him making off with that spoon.'

'He stole it?'

'Not exactly. The trouble was your uncle wanted to try again. He was bewitched by that spoon. But your dad had seen how close we'd come to disaster, so he ran off with it and hid it somewhere in the factory. Your uncle blew his top. He demanded your dad give it back, but he didn't.

'Percy turned this place upside down looking for the spoon. But he never found it. He was so cross with your dad, he packed him off to boarding school and we never saw him again.'

I felt a surge of anger. What a bully. No wonder Dad changed his name.

Ernie sighed. 'Percy wrote to your dad and said he could come back if he told him where the spoon was, but your dad never did. And I'm glad. Though I did miss Timmy very much.'

'And I missed you, too,' said a familiar voice.

It was Dad. (True bug men are always stealthy.)

Ernie went red. 'I'm sorry, Timmy – I shouldn't have told him.'

But Dad just smiled. He sat down next to us and patted Ernie on the shoulder. 'Don't worry,' he said gently. 'He'd have found out sooner or later.'

For the first time, I saw the faint scars on the inside of my dad's arms – his porridge burns. I'm embarrassed to say I'd never noticed them before. I looked at him with new eyes. To me, he'd always been a bit of a clown. A silly old bloke in brown cords who spent too much time with slugs. Now I realised he was actually a hero.

Ernie grinned. 'Did you find anything interesting in the gardens?'

'Loads. Some really good worms. They're quite rare. I'll bring some specimen jars with me tomorrow.'

'Tomorrow?' I said.

Dad nodded. 'I want to come back and have a proper look round the place, and go through the books with Ernie.'

'Does that mean you're not selling Piddler's?' I suddenly felt a spark of hope.

'I honestly don't know,' sighed Dad. 'Mr Snoodle knows more about business than I do. If he thinks he can turn a profit at Piddler's, well, maybe he can.'

Ernie's lips tightened. 'He certainly knows how to cut jobs. I've seen him cut his own factory back to the bone.'

I looked around at the cheery-faced porridgers and felt a sick feeling in my stomach. I didn't want them to lose their jobs. I didn't want Piddler's to change. And then another thought burst into my brain. If Snoodle *did* buy the factory, then he'd get his hands on the Spoon of Doom. And if he used it, and it all went haywire like the last time, well, we could all end up drowning in noodles…

I gulped. I liked Snoodle's Noodles. But not *that* much. Suddenly, I was scanning the canteen and wondering where it was. Where had Dad put it? Somewhere in this dark crumbly old factory was a potential weapon of mass destruction. Heck! It had almost turned my uncle Percy into a 'cereal killer'.

# Chapter Ten

You're probably wondering why I didn't just ask Dad where it was. Well, I did. In the car on the way back home. But he said it was such a long time ago that he couldn't actually remember what he'd done with it.

I didn't believe a word. But I knew better than to try to winkle it out of him. (Bug men are exceptionally stubborn.)

None of us said much more on the subject when we got home, and after a quick tea (fish fingers), I was happy to head for bed.

But I couldn't sleep. I kept thinking about that spoon. What would have happened if Dad hadn't stopped it? Maybe he and Ernie would have drowned – and Uncle Percy and the porridgers, too – and then eventually a tidal wave of grey gunge would have burst out of the factory and thundered down onto the town below, smothering people as they slept; a lethal helping of 'breakfast in bed'.

I shuddered. What a way to go. I imagined divers visiting our town years later, finding bones and skulls and one perfect spoon…

Eventually, I drifted off to sleep, but I still dreamed of Piddler's – the clanking din of the bobbing tins and the throat-choking pong of porridge.

As a result, Sunday started long before I was ready to face it. In fact, I was still sound asleep when the sun's long fingers poked me sharply in the eye. I winced and pulled the duvet over my head, and would happily have stayed there all morning if Mum hadn't appeared.

'Get out of bed, beetle head!' she said throwing back the covers. 'It's a beautiful sunny day, and I'm dying to show you the spiders at Piddler's.'

As if that would entice me out of bed. But I knew it was pointless arguing. And after a quick breakfast (toast and jam, not porridge, thank goodness), we were back at the factory.

But this time Dad was a different man. He strode through the gate like he owned the place – heck! He *did* own the place.

Mum was cheery, too. She and Dad were both hoping to do a spot of bug-bothering before they got down to the serious stuff of looking at the books.

I spotted Ernie waving to us from the car park. Then I noticed he wasn't alone.

'I hope you don't mind,' he said, striding over swinging his enormous arms, 'but I brought my granddaughter with me. I thought she'd be company for Albert.'

I groaned. It was Mandy Moon from school. (You'll remember Mandy – she was the girl at school who threw a wobbly when the marsh slug appeared on my cheese-and-pickle roll.) I hadn't twigged that she was Ernie's granddaughter.

To be perfectly honest, I wasn't overly thrilled to see her. Don't get me wrong – I've nothing against girls. Some of my best friends are girls. (Actually they're not. They're called Colin and Barry, and they'd both punch me on the nose if I called them girls.) But Mandy is a real girly girl. All fluff-puff and sparkle dust. Everything about her is pink. Even her pencils have pink fluffy tops on them. And she's a real moan-athon, too.

We eyed each other dubiously. But my parents didn't notice. They were too busy unpacking their bug kits – specimen jars, magnifying glasses, small shiny trowels…

Dad was especially excited. 'I think I spotted a gobbler worm yesterday,' he said, grinning. 'They're amazing, Albert. They can demolish food faster than me.'

(Actually, that did sound impressive. Dad's appetite was legendary – especially for doughnuts.)

'It's just a shame they don't breed well, because they'd make brilliant composters…'

Then I glazed over like I always do when Dad starts talking about bugs. And I was glad when Mum suggested the rest of us head indoors. I was desperate to do some searching, too.

But not for bugs.

You see, in the car on the way to Piddler's I'd made a decision – I had to find that spoon. I just couldn't help myself. I had to see it. Hold it. (And definitely keep it out of Smedley Snoodle's sticky fingers.) But as I looked up at the crumbly old factory, wondering where to start searching, I suddenly felt a shiver run down my back. I had the distinct feeling we were being watched.

I scanned the windows, but saw nothing. Then I cursed myself. Piddler's wasn't open on a Sunday. And Smedley Snoodle wasn't likely to have a key. Still, I couldn't shake off the feeling that somewhere inside the walls of Piddler's was someone, or *something*, that was keeping a close eye on everything we were doing.

Distinguished jumping spiders don't jump. Actually, that's a fib. They *do* jump – otherwise they'd have an even sillier name than me. But the spiders Mum took us to see didn't jump. I think it was the shock of four pairs of eyes peering down at them that put them off.

We were all up on Piddler's roof. Me, Mum, Ernie and Mandy. (Dad was burrowing for gobbler worms in the factory gardens down below.) What a mess – a big crumbly jungle of rubble, moss and weeds. Obviously just the sort of place a rare spider would choose to set up home.

Mum was crouched down next to a pile of bricks, halfway through telling us a hundred and forty-two things she felt we really needed to know about rare arachnids ... when Mandy suddenly said she felt sick.

I tried not to laugh. You see, Mandy often does this at school. Usually when it's gym. Or maths. Or anything else she'd really rather not do. Whenever she gets the slightest bit bored, she clutches her belly, sticks out her tongue, and starts moaning. Mrs Cooper, our teacher, says she's got a bright future ahead of her ... on the stage.

For once I was grateful, because I was bored, too.

Luckily, Mum was far too interested in the spiders to see through Mandy's little act. And nor did Ernie (though I suspect he was secretly quite glad to escape the spiders as well). He suggested Mandy have a lie down in Uncle Percy's office.

As sick bays go, it wouldn't be my first choice. Not with that whopping great picture of stern-faced old Uncle Percy peering down at you from the wall. But Mandy was keen. So that was settled.

'You go with them,' Mum said to me. 'I won't be long – I just need to take a few more specimens.'

Bugs always come before bodies in our house.

So me and Ernie carted off poor pink moaning Mandy. (Really, she could win an Oscar and she's only ten.)

As we approached Uncle Percy's office, Mandy's moaning increased in volume and dropped in tone. To be honest, she was beginning to sound alarmingly like an old bloke ... when suddenly I realised it *was* an old bloke.

'Dad!'

Mandy was instantly forgotten. Because lying sprawled on the floor of Uncle Percy's office was my dad, and he had a giant gash across his forehead. Next to him was that ugly old picture of Percy, its frame slightly broken down one edge.

I don't like blood. And I very nearly did a 'Mandy'.

'Albert!' gasped Dad, his eyes flickering open briefly. 'It's gone. The Spoon of Doom has gone!'

# Chapter Eleven

Dad passed out fairly quickly after we arrived, but not before explaining what had happened.

He told us how he'd sneaked back to the office to make sure the spoon was where he'd left it, all those years ago, taped to the inside of that giant old picture frame.

'I thought I could reach it without a chair,' whispered Dad, 'but the picture fixings were rusty – the blooming thing fell on my head.' He grimaced as a fat finger of blood oozed from his forehead.

I tried not to look, but Ernie was obviously made of stronger stuff (*Piddler's Pride*, no doubt), because he took out his hanky (porridge grey) and pressed it firmly onto the wound.

Dad winced and bit his lip, then seemed to recover a bit. 'The spoon was there, Albert, I saw it, exactly where I'd left it. I reached out and touched it, but then everything went black. And when I woke up, it was gone.'

Gone?

Dad grimaced again. 'I think someone took it.'

Ernie gasped. 'Who was it, Timmy?'

Dad shook his head. 'I don't know – I was probably dreaming, but I think I saw that noodle man.'

'Smedley Snoodle?' I gasped.

But Dad didn't answer. He'd conked out.

Ernie shook his head angrily. 'So Snoodle *did* know about the spoon!' he growled. 'I thought as much. He obviously followed your dad in here and swiped it when the picture fell on his head.'

I felt an angry knot growing in my tummy. I *knew* someone had been watching us. It must have been him. He must have broken into Piddler's and waited for us to come back – knowing that my dad would try and retrieve the spoon...

It was Mandy who dialled 999. Me and Ernie were still too shocked to move. But Mandy suddenly seemed to have morphed into Wonder Woman. (Wonder Woman wearing a pink fluffy skirt, pink top and matching boots.) Her sickness stunt forgotten, she not only called the ambulance, she also covered Dad with one of Percy's old bed blankets and then went to get Mum.

Meanwhile, I was seething. (I must admit I am a

bit of a hothead sometimes. Mum says I look like a stag beetle when I'm cross because I've got short black hair that stands up on end. It was certainly standing up now.) I clenched my fists and gritted my teeth. That spoon belonged to us. Whether we used it or not was *our* business – Piddler's business. It had nothing to do with that Snoodle man. And what if *he* decided to use it? Anything could happen…

I wished I had a pair of thundering forearms to go and shake at him. Then I made up my mind – big arms or not, I was going to get our spoon back. By whatever means necessary.

When the ambulance men arrived on the scene, Dad came round and said he was feeling better, but his face was white and he was shivering with cold.

They loaded him onto a stretcher and Mum said she'd go along to the hospital. Ernie offered to take me home.

As they were about to carry him away, Dad beckoned me over.

'Did you see the worm, Albert?'

I shook my head.

'I had it with me – a giant gobbler it was – in a specimen jar. It's amazing, Albert, you have to see it…'

(That was typical of Dad. Even with a giant hole in his head he was still blethering about bugs.)

'But I can't seem to find it, Albert,' he gasped, looking around the room weakly. Then suddenly he struggled against the stretcher, as if he was trying to sit up to get a better look.

'I'll find it, Dad,' I promised, pressing him back down. 'You just get better, OK.'

After they'd gone, I looked around the room. But I couldn't see any worm. And to be honest, I didn't give it much thought, because I had something else on my mind…

The spoon.

*The Spoon of Doom.*

Seeing Dad lying on that stretcher had made me all the more determined to reclaim what was ours. But as I closed Uncle Percy's office door, I suddenly wondered whether that spoon was already casting its shadow on anyone who touched it. I shuddered. Dad had found it again, and look what had happened to him.

# Chapter Twelve

Getting the spoon back definitely wasn't going to be easy. For a start, the Snoodle's Noodles factory wasn't a bit like Piddler's. It was small and swanky, with cross-looking blokes in blue uniforms guarding the gates.

The crossest of them all was now blocking my way, clipboard and pen in hand. 'I've told you three times, sonny, you're not on my list. And if you're not on my list, you don't get in. Now clear off.'

I very nearly did. I'm ashamed to say my anger had evaporated. And I suddenly felt very small standing there in front of Snoodle's Noodles. After all, what could I say? *Please can I have my spoon back?* It wasn't exactly a football that I'd kicked into Snoodle's back garden.

'This isn't working, Albert,' said a moany voice next to me.

Mandy Moon.

I didn't want to bring her. But she made me.

You see, while Ernie went off to make sure everything was locked, I'd decided to sneak off and pay Snoodle a visit. But I got as far as Piddler's front door when…

'Where are you going?' Mandy asked.

We were both supposed to be waiting in reception while Ernie did his rounds.

I hesitated for a heartbeat. 'Next door,' I whispered, glancing down the corridor in case Ernie reappeared.

'Can I come?'

'No! Definitely not.'

**66**

Mandy made a face. 'GRANDAD!' she yelped.

'Be quiet,' I shushed.

'Not unless I can come.' She folded her arms and scowled at me. 'Because if this is Piddler's business, I should be involved, too.'

I glared at her. 'Why?'

'Because I'm a porridger – or probably will be one day.'

I looked at her as if she was off her head.

She scowled at me. 'It's not just my grandad that works here, Albert,' she snapped. 'So do my parents. And my big brother. And all my aunts and uncles. My family has always worked here. And, anyway, I know more about the Spoon of Doom than you do. All of us porridgers do.'

I looked at Mandy closely. She didn't look like she was descended from a long line of porridgers. Her forearms were skinnier than mine.

'So, if everyone knows about the spoon,' I snapped. 'Why don't I?' (And the rest of the world for that matter. Why weren't there Indiana Jones lookalikes swinging from the banisters trying to get their hands on it at that very moment?)

'Not *everyone* knows about the spoon,' she said crossly. 'Only the porridgers. And we never share Piddler's secrets outside the factory.'

It was like some crazy code of conduct. A porridge pledge, or something.

'But what I don't understand,' said Mandy, 'is why you want it back. If this Snoodle man has got it, let him have it.'

Sometimes girls are very stupid.

'It's our spoon,' I snapped. 'He stole it. People can't just go around stealing things. And anyway, what if he uses it – do you really want to be smothered to death by *Kebab 'n' Ketchup* instant noodles?'

But it didn't matter anyway, because we'd already fallen at the first fence. There we were standing outside the Snoodle's Noodles factory with no earthly chance of being allowed in.

'If you don't go now, I'll call the police!' bellowed the grumpy uniform.

I was about to start begging for an appointment, when things got a million times worse.

Mandy suddenly gripped my arm, squeezed it hard and started yowling at the top of her voice. 'Albert! Albert!' she squealed. 'I don't feel well.'

I cringed. Not now. Not here… But Mandy had turned white. She'd started shaking all over. Any moment, she looked like she might fall over. I felt like crying.

Then she clasped her hand to her mouth and

said very loudly, 'I think I'm going to be sick.'

The security guard gawped at us. 'What's wrong with her?'

'She's just a bit off-colour,' I said through gritted teeth. I turned on her with a face like thunder.

But then she winked at me. It was definitely a wink.

'Oh, Albert,' she was screaming now. 'I think I'm going to barf.'

'Water,' I said loudly. 'She needs water!'

A bustle of blue uniforms appeared from the little office next to the gates, and Mandy was now hysterical; rolling around on the ground as if her insides were about to burst out.

And then I had my chance.

The security guards were swarming round Mandy, like ants round a jam jar. And not one of them noticed me slip through the gates, pad across the perimeter and make my way swiftly to the very heart of the Snoodle's Noodles Empire.

I remember reading somewhere that if you walk purposefully, no one will stop you. (It always seems to work in films.) So that's what I did. My heart was pumping. My pulse was racing. At any moment I expected to feel a hand on my shoulder.

But I didn't.

I walked straight past the very efficient-looking reception team (even on a Sunday there was no slacking – and certainly no knitting – at Snoodle's) and headed for the first corridor I saw.

Of course, I had no idea where I was going. If I'd been in Piddler's, I'd immediately have come a cropper, because there are no signs and no rhyme or reason to the layout of the porridge plant. It's as if they're preparing for a siege and don't want the invaders to have any clues as to how to find the porridge room. But the Snoodle's Noodles factory was a model of efficiency. On the wall to my right was a neat, easy-to-follow floorplan. And two minutes later I took a deep breath and marched straight into the exceedingly plush offices of Mr Smedley Snoodle himself. (Really, they could make it a bit harder. After all, I could have been a disgruntled customer, dissatisfied at the amount of onion in my *Onion Bhaji Noodle Doodle*, and ready to have it out with the big boss man himself.)

To say Mr Snoodle was shocked was an understatement. He nearly choked on his lunch.

'What do you want?' he spluttered, spitting out chunks of noodle across his desk.

I was shocked, too. I didn't realise that food magnates ate their own stuff. You'd think they'd be cheesed off with it after making the stuff for so many years. Heck! I never wanted to eat porridge and I'd only been at Piddler's ten minutes...

Snoodle glared at me. But he wasn't the only one. A pointy-nosed woman was there as well.

'You can't come in here,' she gasped, her mouth also full of noodles.

'I want my spoon back,' I squeaked. 'It's Piddler's property, and you stole it.'

'I don't know what you're talking about,' Snoodle snapped back.

I glanced quickly around the room to see if I could spot it. The place was a shrine to the world of instant noodles. There were posters. And pots. And packets and pans. And even a large cardboard cutout of Smedley Snoodle sucking up one exceedingly long noodle.

But no spoon.

On the desk was an enormous map (now covered in half-chewed noodle), and propped up against it were two tall fishing rods.

But still no spoon.

'I've no idea how you got in here,' snarled Smedley. 'But heads will roll!'

I suddenly started to feel scared. After all, ten-year-old boys don't normally find themselves confronting noodle barons.

'Please,' I said, my voice quivering. 'Just give me back my spoon, and I'll go.'

Smedley looked like he'd explode. 'Will you stop squawking about spoons! Really, we don't know what you're talking about.'

But then I spotted Miss Pointy Nose furtively shoving something under the map – something big and bulky…

Something obviously spoon-shaped…

I made a grab.

'Aha!' I said, my spunk returning.

But unfortunately it wasn't the spoon. It was a specimen box. Just like the ones my dad used. And inside, wriggling around, was an enormous worm.

And then a klaxon went off in my brain again. *This* must be the worm my dad had found that morning. The worm he'd been telling me about when they were stretchering him away – the gobbler worm. The worm that could eat as much as he could...

'I can explain...' said Miss Pointy Nose.

But Smedley Snoodle shook his head and turned to me himself. His manner had changed. He flashed a very insincere smile.

'You seem to have caught us out, young Grub.' He coughed. 'You see, my assistant Pamela and I paid a visit to your father this morning, to have an informal word with him about selling the factory to us...'

'Because of the spoon?'

Snoodle frowned. 'What? No! This has nothing to do with cutlery. I want Piddler's for the *land*. I'm planning a massive expansion programme. The future is noodle-shaped, young Grub. Microwave meals in minutes.' He scrabbled around in a drawer for a bit, then tossed a pile of papers at me.

'I have plans … architect's drawings … I want to knock down Piddler's and build the biggest noodle factory in the world.'

'Not on your Nelly noodle!' A loud, high-pitched squeal suddenly burst into the room.

It was Mandy Moon, surrounded by security guards who were trying to grab her flailing arms. For someone so skinny, she was doing a very good job of fending them off.

'I presume she's with you?' said Snoodle, rolling his eyes.

I wished I could say no.

'We'll never let you knock Piddler's down,' shouted Mandy. 'Will we, Albert?'

I was about to agree, but Snoodle beat me to it…

'I can and *will* knock it down,' he snapped. 'Once your father sees sense and sells it to me. How is his head, by the way? When we arrived, he appeared to be in a bit of a bad way…'

I scowled at them. After all, they hadn't even bothered calling for help. Instead, they'd left my dad to bleed to death all over Uncle Percy's carpet. Besides, I'd heard enough. If Snoodle had the spoon, he certainly wasn't about to show it to me. I turned to go, when suddenly I remembered something…

'What about the worm? Why did you pinch that?'

Snoodle and his assistant smiled sheepishly at one another.

'Fishing,' chuckled Snoodle. 'My secret hobby, Grub. It's how I relax and unwind. You should try it.' He grinned at his assistant again. 'Pamela thought the worm might make good bait.'

I was appalled. I'm no bug-botherer, but still, I had standards. I snatched up the specimen box. 'It's Piddler's property,' I said firmly, slipping it into my coat pocket. And with my head held high, I turned and fled. Closely followed by Mandy Moon.

# Chapter Thirteen

'So if he hasn't got it, who has?' panted Mandy, running to keep up with me.

I shrugged. 'I don't know, but if we don't get back to Piddler's quickly your grandad will have called out a search party.'

I needn't have worried. Ernie hadn't even noticed we'd been away. Mandy and I got back to reception just as he appeared from the bowels of the plant, red faced and flustered.

'Sorry, kids,' he puffed. 'I've been trying to find the generator keys. Some idiot has turned on Old Bertha and locked the room – and the key isn't where it should be.'

But I wasn't listening. I was too busy thinking about Smedley Snoodle and wondering whether he was telling the truth or not. I had my doubts. And if he was lying and he *did* have the spoon, our town could very soon be smothered in a smog of Snoodle's Noodles. I shuddered at the thought.

'I've got something for you, Albert,' said Ernie, as he led us out to his car. 'I found it in your uncle's office.'

He handed me a book. Brown and damp. And well thumbed. *Frederick Funnel's Book of Fantastic Phantasms.* It didn't look promising.

I turned a few pages and wrinkled my nose. It smelt awful. Like a wet dog. Or a dead dog. Or a wet, dead dog.

'I know it's in a bit of a state,' said Ernie, reversing carefully out of the car park. 'But it's got a paragraph or two on the Spoon.'

And just as Ernie said the word 'spoon', the book fell open at the appropriate page.

I'm not superstitious. Not in the slightest. I don't generally cower at black cats, and I'm happy to walk under, over, up, down or any which way you like, around a ladder. But even I felt a slight shiver sprint up my spine. I glanced at the page.

*The Spoon of Doom was never meant to feed the needy, but to serve up grief to the mean and greedy.*

'Let me see,' said Mandy, peering over my shoulder. But I shrugged her off.

*The spoon is believed to have belonged to Meg Muldoon, a witch who was burned at the stake in Shrewsbury in 1649.*

I momentarily lost my place, as a sleek black sports car pulled out in front of us and Ernie slammed on the brakes.

'Snoodle,' snapped Ernie. 'Curse that man!'

I read on…

*The spoon was said to be possessed by evil spirits and was used by Meg to mix up her foul potions.*

*Before she was burned, Meg cursed those who condemned her and said that anyone who used the spoon would be smothered alive.*

*Her curse came true. After the burning, when the sticks on her pyre were still smouldering and spitting, a 'calamitous commotion' ensued in the White Swan public house in Shrewsbury Square, whereby several people drowned in a fast-flowing barrel of ale.*

I gasped. So the Spoon of Doom was a witch's spoon…

*Reports thereafter are sketchy, but years later the spoon reappeared. It was referred to in an account of the sinking of a cargo ship the* Sally Ann, *which sunk off Shutter's Reef, Lundy, with all hands lost in 1724. One passenger, a trader named Ling, survived to bring word of the wreck. And he talked of a hellish spoon that had flooded the ship's galley and caused the ship to flounder.*

'Anyone for fish and chips?' said Ernie cheerfully. 'We could stop off on the way home.'

I nodded, but carried on reading…

*The spoon appears to have been recovered; it is mentioned again in the journals of Samuel Boden, a merchant who travelled in Russia in the nineteenth century. In a letter to his sister, he writes of visiting a ruined village in the Urals, which had been swallowed up by a foul swamp of rotten oatmeal that locals blamed on a cursed spoon.*

Could that have been the village Uncle Percy's man had visited?

'Peas or beans, Albert?'

We'd stopped outside the Fry & Buy (the town chippy).

'Pickled onions for me,' chirped Mandy.

'Anything,' I said.

(Anything as long as it wasn't served with a spoon.)

Mum was home by the time they dropped me off. She was out watering Dad's bugs (soft bellies like it soggy). She smiled when she saw me.

'Dad's going to be fine,' she beamed. 'He's got a bit of a headache and needs to stay in overnight so they can keep an eye on him. But he's definitely on the mend.'

It was good news. And suddenly I felt like a weight had been lifted from my shoulders. It didn't matter about the spoon, or Snoodle, so long as Dad was going to be OK.

Then Mum ruined it all.

'But your dad and I have been talking, Albert, and we both think we should sell Piddler's to Mr Snoodle.'

*What?*

'But you can't,' I gasped.

I suddenly thought of Ernie and the porridgers, and Snoodle's plans to flatten the factory so he could build his own super-sized noodle plant.

Mum plonked a pile of lettuce on the ground for the slugs, and shrugged.

'I know it seems a bit hasty…'

A bit?

'And in some ways I'd like to keep the factory. But your dad's just not comfortable there.'

I grimaced. After everything Dad had been through with his uncle and the spoon, I could sort of understand his feelings. But still…

'Anyway,' said Mum, tossing more lettuce on the ground, 'we're not business people. The factory needs an expert in charge.'

'But *I* could run it,' I yelped.

(OK, I couldn't. But maybe Ernie could?)

'No, you can't, Albert. You've got school…

Hey! Watch out,' she squeaked, leaping forward to retrieve a small snail that was a wiggle away from my left foot. She put down the snail in a safer part of the swamp and headed for the worms.

I chased after her, trying not to squish any more squashy stuff.

'But, Mum,' I said desperately, 'Snoodle just wants to knock Piddler's down to build a bigger noodle factory.'

'You don't know that,' said Mum firmly. Then she softened and sighed. 'Look, I know you're excited about Piddler's, but kids change their minds. Next week you might be more interested in brain surgery … or being a bin man … or you might grow to love bugs like us.'

Never. No way. Not Ever.

'Oh, look,' she said, suddenly pointing at a scuttling bug. 'It's a tortoise beetle.'

I rolled my eyes and gritted my teeth. It's useless trying to have a serious conversation with anyone the slightest bit interested in bugs. They're just so easily distracted. Instead, I slunk off to my bedroom. I'd intended to read more of that book, but as soon as my head hit the pillow, I crashed out.

And that's how I stayed until the bullet hit my window.

The assassin was small and pink. And exceedingly moany.

'Albert! Albert Grub! Get up. I need you.'

*What*? I sat up, as another bullet chipped the glass.

'Grub,' shrieked the voice again. 'Come on!'

It felt like one of those nightmares that are so real you can touch them. And then I realised it wasn't bullets hitting my window, it was stones. (Actually it was snail shells. That's all Mandy could find. But empty ones, of course.)

'What do you want?' I growled, as I thrust my head out the window. (Honestly, why don't people ever knock on doors in times of trouble?)

'There's something happening at Piddler's,' she shrieked in a sort of high-pitched stage whisper, which I reckoned the whole street could hear. 'Grandad's gone up there. And I think he might be in trouble.'

I didn't have time to dress. I just pulled on my coat over my PJs and found my shoes. Of course, what I *should* have done is wake Mum and get her to drive us. But if there was a problem at Piddler's, I didn't want her to know about it. (I didn't want to give her any more excuses to flog our inheritance.)

In five minutes I was on my bike, trying to keep up with Mandy.

'Grandad phoned my parents,' she yelled, pedalling manically in front. 'He saw smoke coming from Piddler's chimney, and he's gone to check it out.'

'Why didn't he call us?' I puffed. After all, we were legally in charge now.

'He didn't want to worry your mum – what with your dad taking a tumble and all… Can't you pedal any faster, Albert?'

No, I couldn't. I am not a born cyclist. Mandy, on the other hand, looked like she was in the Tour de France. I think she secretly has a pair of porridger's legs, rather than the usual forearms.

It was all uphill, but eventually we arrived at the front gate of the factory. In the darkness it looked terrifying. People say old houses are scary at night. They might be. But this was something else. The dark bulk of the building loomed over us. And I'm ashamed to say that I nearly turned tail and cycled home. I realised then that I am not brave. Not at all. And I was just about to suggest to Mandy that we'd be better off coming back in the morning, when I suddenly spotted a light.

'What's that?' I whispered.

Mandy peered into the darkness. 'That's the porridge room,' she said.

At the far end of the factory, in the part that overlooked the town, there was definitely something going on inside. Then...

'Listen,' Mandy said.

I gasped. 'Old Bertha?'

She nodded.

We could hear the heavy drone of Piddler's generator, and a strange sensation gripped my knees. I felt cold and hot at the same time.

'I think someone's using the spoon,' I said quietly.

Mandy frowned and then, without another word, she threw down her bike and began climbing over the gate.

'Come on, Albert,' she bellowed. 'My grandad's in there.'

Reluctantly, I followed. By the time I'd got one leg over the top of the gate, Mandy was already bounding up the path, heading for the doors.

'Grandad!' she shouted, rattling them madly. 'GRANDAD!'

I caught up with her, panting and breathless. My heart was racing. My hands felt sweaty. Something or *someone* bad was inside the factory. I could feel it.

# Chapter Fourteen

The doors were locked.

'Is there another way in?' I said, trying to sound keen. Really, I'd have preferred to scarper while we still had the chance.

Mandy shrugged. 'I'm not sure. One of the canteen windows, maybe…'

I followed her round the side of the factory.

She peered up. 'That one,' she said, pointing out a particularly puny-looking window. 'It's got a rotten frame.'

I wasn't quite sure what she had in mind.

'Come on, Albert. Stick a brick through it!'

What? Who did she think I was?

'Just wrap your coat round your hand and you won't cut yourself.'

How did she know how to break a window?

Mandy frowned. 'Don't you watch telly?'

I didn't think now was the time to tell her about our telly – the fuzzy picture makes it difficult to see anything most of the time. Instead, I grabbed the brick, closed my eyes and went for it.

Of course it worked.

'I'll go through,' said Mandy, shoving me aside. 'I'm smaller than you.'

I'm glad she did – the edges were razor sharp, but somehow Mandy wriggled through without so much as snagging her perfect pink tights.

'I'm in,' she said dropping to the ground. 'I'll open the kitchen door for you.'

Piddler's really was a disgrace. No security system. No security guards. Not even any decent windows. Mind you – who'd want to steal a pile of porridge?

'Come on, Albert,' said Mandy, as I followed her inside. 'We've got to find Grandad.'

I didn't think that would be a problem. I knew exactly where he'd be.

'The porridge room,' I said quietly.

Mandy froze. 'You're not saying Grandad's involved in all of this?'

Of course I wasn't. Well, not really. But someone had the spoon, I was sure of it. And by now I reckoned poor old Ernie Moon was probably up to his neck in *Piddler's Pride*.

It's a good job Mandy knew her way round. I wouldn't have had a clue how to find the porridge room. We tiptoed down the dark corridors until we reached the place with the overalls. And then, with a deep breath and a pounding heart, we pushed open the doors.

I blinked at the light. White light, burning bright. And then the smell hit me like a wall. I struggled to breathe.

The factory was running at full pelt. Thousands of tins were thundering along the conveyor belt, each fighting for their turn under the enormous porridge pot. Through the steam, I could vaguely see Ernie, running wildly around the room, his arms full of tins. He was struggling to keep up, and puddles of porridge covered the conveyor belt.

Then I looked up to the gantry, and my heart missed a beat. Because there, standing stirring the enormous porridge pot, was the skeletal ghost of Percival Piddler himself.

My mouth turned dry and I swallowed a scream. I wanted to run away, but my legs wouldn't work. And then his black eyes locked onto mine.

'But you're dead!' I gasped.

The ghost grinned and gave a horrible cackle.

I shuddered. It had no teeth. (Mind you, dead men don't need a good set of gnashers.)

'Get out of here!' shouted Ernie, from the other side of the floor. 'Get out, while you still can.'

But my legs wouldn't work.

Mandy's did. But she didn't escape. Instead, she scrambled over to Ernie and started loading tins.

It wasn't enough. Hot porridge was pouring onto the floor; a steaming carpet of bubbling breakfast gunk. And still I couldn't take my eyes off the phantom porridger. Then suddenly I came to my senses. Dead men don't make porridge. This was no ghost. This was Percy Piddler himself.

A current of crossness crackled through my bones. 'It was all a lie!' I shouted at him. (Extra loud in case he was hard of hearing.) 'You tricked us all – just to get your hands on that stupid spoon.'

He didn't deny it. He just grinned back at me.

And then I was off. I hurled myself across the factory floor, slipping and skidding on the porridge, which was lapping against the walls, and still rising. I took the steps two at a time, and suddenly I was standing before him on the gantry. He didn't look scary any more. He was just a super-skinny old man. (With a spoon.)

Cross as I was, I couldn't help but peer into the porridge pot next to him. I gasped. I had to admit it was amazing. Not to look at, of course. Nope. It looked just like any other bog-standard wooden spoon you'd pick up for a pound in a bargain basement. But amazingly it was stirring the pot all by itself. I couldn't take my eyes off it. Round and round. Faster and faster. And the quicker it stirred, the more porridge it made.

'You've got to stop it,' shouted Ernie from down below. 'We've run out of tins and we haven't got any buckets big enough. Please, Percy – stop it.'

'Never!' growled Percy. 'It's my spoon. It's my factory. And if I want to fill it with porridge, I will.'

See – mad. Mad as cheese. I'm never sure how to treat mad people. Is it best to go along with them? Agree with them? Make helpful suggestions? Or tell them straight? I opted for the latter.

'But you won't have a factory left if you don't stop that spoon.'

Percy Piddler scowled at me. 'I don't care. I'm 98.' (As if that made it OK.)

'Well, if *you* won't stop it, *I* will,' I said, trying to sound manly, though I didn't feel it.

I eyed the steaming pot nervously. I don't know how my dad found the courage to stick his hand inside, all those years ago. From where I was standing, the spoon was spinning so fast it looked like it would chop my hands off in an instant. (See. I'm no bug man – I'm not the slightest bit brave.)

And still the porridge flowed.

Ernie was now standing in a sea of the stuff, trying to stop himself from being swept away. Mandy had climbed on top of a pallet of *Piddler's Pride* and was yelling her head off. And then there was a crash, and I turned to see one of the large glass windows at the end of the factory shatter, and the porridge begin pushing outside.

'You'll flood the town, Percy,' shouted Ernie. 'Think of the people.'

'I *am* thinking of them,' growled Percy. 'They'll wake up with breakfast in bed!

Another window crashed, and *still* the pot kept pumping out porridge.

I looked at the spoon and felt my stomach twist. There was nothing else for it. Just as my dad had done, I'd have to stick my hand in that boiling pot and stop it myself.

But as I reached forward, another thought burst into my brain. I've no idea how. Or why. But I suddenly remembered Dad's worm. Perhaps bug men are telepathic and Dad was somehow helping me – or more likely the porridge pong was getting to me again – but suddenly a vision of that worm popped into my head. What was it Dad had called it – a *gobbler* worm. A worm with as good an appetite as him…

I felt in my coat pocket. Yep, it was still there where I'd stuffed it after I'd left Snoodle's office. I pulled out the box and peered at the worm. It was certainly big. And horrible looking. And then a tiny spark of an idea took shape. If this worm really had an appetite, could it eat porridge? Bucket-loads of porridge… A factory full of porridge? Not on its own, of course, but maybe with a little help from some friends?

I didn't stop to think things through. With a silent apology to the worm for its brave sacrifice, I tossed it into the porridge pot and closed my eyes.

# Chapter Fifteen

'What are you doing?' screamed Percy.

I hardly dared look.

There was a hiss. And a thump. And a loud bang. And the spoon suddenly stopped, like someone had stuck a stick in the spokes of a wheel. For a moment I actually thought that one worm (a wonder worm perhaps) had somehow stopped the spoon. But no. After missing a beat, the spoon slowly started stirring again. Round and round. Up and down. Faster and faster...

My heart sank. I'd murdered the worm for absolutely no reason. How would I face Dad? Then suddenly there was a high-pitched squeal from down below.

'Worms!' screamed Mandy.

I peered over the edge of the gantry, and watched as the porridge pot started squirting out porridge again, but this porridge was different. It was still the same grey gunk, but each squirt also contained a handful of big fat gobbler worms.

The spoon was still making porridge, but it was also making worms – *hundreds* of worms!

Percy's eyes were out on stalks. 'What have you done?' he screamed. 'My lovely porridge.'

We both stared down at the scene below.

Ernie was now standing in a writhing, wriggling mess of porridge and worms. And still more of them blobbed out.

'They're gobbler worms, Ernie,' I yelled down. 'We won't drown in porridge – they'll swallow the stuff.' (I was crossing my fingers behind my back at this point. Because to be perfectly honest, I hadn't really been paying attention to my dad's description of the qualities of the gobbler worm.)

'But who'll eat the worms?' Ernie yelled back, ever so slightly cross sounding.

I hadn't thought of that.

The floor was now choked in slimy pink bodies. I'm pretty bug-hardened myself, but even *my* stomach heaved.

'You've ruined everything,' moaned Old Percy next to me. 'How could you...'

And without another word, he reached over and stuck his own hands into that menacing pot of boiling porridge. His screams reverberated around the room as he wrestled with the spoon, and then finally pulled the thing out and threw it to the gantry floor.

I expected it to writhe or wiggle like a thing possessed. But it didn't. It just lay there. Spoon-like.

After that things slowed down slightly. The porridge pot stopped, and so did the worm production. Ernie was able to wade over and rescue Mandy.

Meanwhile, Percy sank to his knees and clutched his chest. 'I don't feel well,' he gasped.

I wasn't surprised – his arms were red and shiny and starting to blister. But that didn't stop him scowling at Ernie as he and Mandy clambered onto the gantry.

'I tried to stop him…' panted Ernie, his clothes sodden with porridge and great globules of wriggling gobbler worms. 'But he'd locked the generator room, so I couldn't turn it off. And by the time I got in here, he was already up to his ankles in porridge.'

Old Percy scowled. 'You should have left me alone. Everything was working perfectly well without you.'

Mandy was peering at Percy's arms. 'You need a doctor,' she said firmly, completely ignoring the worms hanging from her hair. 'Grandad, can you give me a piggyback through to reception so we can call an ambulance?'

'Will you be OK?' Ernie asked me.

What could I say? There I was sitting on a metal gantry surrounded by a sea of grey gunk, being slowly scoffed by super-sized worms (or so I hoped), with a mad 98-year-old despot and a satanic spoon. What possible harm could come to me?

'Yep!' I squeaked. 'I'll be fine.'

After they'd gone, I tried not to look at Uncle Percy. His eyes were closed and he was groaning softly to himself. Instead, I stared at the spoon. It looked so ordinary. So … well … wooden. And yet this was Meg Muldoon's spoon. A witch's spoon. It had sunk a ship, smothered a village, and very nearly killed us all. I reached out to touch it.

'Don't!' gasped Percy, suddenly grabbing my wrist. 'That spoon has special powers. Once you've touched it, it takes you over.'

'It didn't take my dad over,' I said, wriggling free of his grasp.

'That's because the skin he touched it with was blistered and peeled.'

I shuddered. Then Percy groaned again. And I couldn't stop myself from asking, 'Why did you do it?'

'*Why*?' he snapped, as if it was me who was doo-lally for not knowing. 'Because I'm a porridge man, of course.' (As if that explained everything.) 'All my life I've been passionate about porridge,' he croaked. 'I was the man who invented lump-free tinned porridge – did you know that?'

I shook my head.

'I invented pilchard porridge – and pineapple-pickle porridge, too – did you know that?'

I didn't.

'And sliced porridge – though that idea never quite took off…'

What could I say – I'd never owned the *Guiness Book of Interesting Facts About Porridge*. (Though I

**98**

suddenly thought I'd quite like to.)

Percy shook his head. 'Then one day porridge went out of fashion, and everyone wanted cornflakes. Cornflakes? Can you believe it?'

I could.

'And then, to make matters worse, the price of oats rocketed. Piddler's very nearly closed. Can you imagine it? A world without Piddler's...'

Actually, I couldn't. Not now.

'Then I read that story about the magic porridge pot ... and they all laughed at me,' Percy growled, looking quite mad again. 'But I had the last laugh, because I found the spoon. The Spoon of Doom – the very spoon that had inspired a thousand stories.'

I looked at the spoon, lying there. And it really didn't look at all inspirational.

'But your father stole it. He never let me see what it was capable of. All these years I've dreamed of seeing what it could do...'

'But you could have flooded the town,' I said, looking around at the current disaster that we were sitting in the middle of.

'Nonsense,' snapped Percy. 'That spoon could have made me a fortune. I could have hired it out to all the other factories in town – dog biscuits, shoe polish, pork pies... Imagine!'

I imagined. I imagined being smothered to death by tins of shoe polish, or pulverised into pieces by a hail of pork pies…

'I turned this place upside down looking for that spoon,' said Percy grimly. 'But I never found it.'

'So you decided to trick my dad into finding it for you,' I said, finally working it out. 'You went on holiday, faked your own death and left everything to Dad, knowing he'd come and remove the spoon?'

Percy winced as the pain in his arms grew worse. 'I knew your father would sell the place if he ever got his hands on it – he's never been interested in the business. But he wouldn't want anyone else to get the spoon. All I had to do was wait and watch…'

So it was Percy who had been boggling us this morning – not Smedley Snoodle. No wonder the noodle baron had thought I was mad, raving on about a spoon.

'But how did you get back from the Alps without anyone spotting you?' I asked.

Percy rolled his eyes as if I was simple.

'Because I didn't go to the Alps. I don't like holidays. I like porridge. I stayed in the factory – there are loads of empty rooms here. I actually slept in my office. No one noticed. And there was plenty of porridge to eat.'

'But what about the lawyer?' I said. 'How did you fool him?'

Percy grinned. 'Cyril Saltman's not really a lawyer, he's an actor. He's also one of my best customers. I offered him a life-time's supply of *Piddler's Pride* in return for him playing the part of my lawyer. All he had to do was tell my staff that I'd died on holiday. Then take my will to your father.'

I frowned. 'But how did you find us?'

'Because your father still sends me a Christmas card every year.'

*What?*

Percy grinned that horrible grin of his. 'Blood is thicker than porridge, Albert. I'm still his uncle.'

I couldn't believe my ears. After everything the old goat had done to him, my dad still sent him a Christmas card. (Blimey – bug men are sentimental.) Then suddenly I noticed Percy's face had changed colour. It looked like prune porridge. Then he let out a strangled gurgle. And died. Honestly. Right there in front of me, he just keeled over and died.

# Chapter Sixteen

Thankfully, the ambulance men arrived just then. And after much chest thumping, and loads of mouth to mouth (rather them than me – Percy had the most awful bad breath and no teeth), they managed to get his heart working again. And, for the second time that day, Percy came back from the dead.

For some reason, I was glad. I even held his hand as we waded through the porridge plant and carried him out to the waiting ambulance.

'What a mess,' said Ernie, as he and Mandy and I watched the blue lights disappear down the hill.

He wasn't wrong. There was porridge everywhere. A big grey puddle of the stuff swept around the front of the factory and oozed down the road, with hundreds of wriggling gobbler worms mingled amongst it.

'At least it didn't reach the town,' said Mandy, casually wiping worms off her collar.

I grinned at Mandy. I was almost starting to like her. (The porridge smell really must have addled my brain.) Then she went and spoilt it all…

'But what a daft idea, Albert,' she frowned. 'I mean, what were you *thinking* about with that worm trick? Did you really think they'd instantly gobble up all the porridge?'

I scowled back at her. When she put it like that, it did sound silly.

Then I heard Ernie sigh deeply. 'What I want to know is what your dad's going to say…'

Then I grinned. Actually, I knew *exactly* what he'd say: 'Fantastic!' He loved bugs. Now he had a factory full of them.

And I was sort of right.

Two days later, Dad returned to Piddler's (his head covered by an enormous invisible-man bandage). And he's barely left the place since.

Neither have I.

I quit school and took over the running of Piddler's and within six months got porridge back on the supermarket shelves. And now every kid in the country tucks into a tin of *Piddler's Pride* for breakfast. (Actually that bit's not true. But it's what I dream about in the bath sometimes.)

But Piddler's *did* become famous. Not for

**103**

porridge. But as a site of scientific interest. Bug-botherers came from all over the world to study the gobbler worms. But unfortunately they weren't the only ones who came. A dozen or so white-suited environmental health honchos also turned up – and closed us down. Apparently porridge and worms don't mix.

Piddler's was finally allowed to reopen. But the clean-up operation – plus the heavy fine it received for having worms in the works – soaked up every penny the business had left in the bank.

Not that Uncle Percy cared. He was a changed man. The fight had finally gone out of him. I'm not sure why. Maybe it was his dicky ticker, or the fact he'd lost most of the skin off his hands (the skin that had touched the spoon). But as soon as he'd recovered, he handed over the porridge plant to Dad and retired. He moved into the Sweet Apple Rest Home, where he was welcomed with open arms, not because of his cheery personality and sunny smile, but because he brought with him trunkfuls of porridge. And as none of the residents had a complete set of gnashers between them, it was a big hit.

Dad's still not sure whether he wants to keep the factory. 'Too many bad memories,' he says.

And it's not as if the place makes much money. Our roof is still leaking and we still can't afford a holiday. But I've made him promise not to sell it, at least not for a bit.

And strangely Mum is on my side. She and Ernie have actually been working on some ideas to expand the Piddler's product range. You see, the moment Mum saw that lake of porridge with the worms wiggling around inside, she had a big idea – breakfast cereals with bugs in them. Or *Grub's Grub* as she calls it.

Don't laugh. I think she's onto something. Bug-botherers will buy anything, so why not a breakfast cereal made just for them?

So far she and Ernie have come up with three ideas:

*Grub's Gruel* – a tinned porridge with chocolate worms mixed in. They're still having a few technical troubles trying to stop the worms from melting in the tins, but it tastes lovely.

Then there are *Beetle-bites* – flakes of corn mixed with bug-shaped raisins. Ernie's not overly keen on that one, mostly because it's got nothing to do with porridge.

And my personal favourite, *Weeta-bugs* – wheat biscuits with jelly ants in the middle.

Look out for them on the supermarket shelves and please buy them. If you don't, Piddler's will probably be flattened to make way for Smedley Snoodle's new noodle plant. (He still comes round regularly to see if Dad's ready to sell. I keep my beady eye on him. Secretly, I think he's just after more gobbler worms for his fishing.)

So that's the story so far. Well, apart from one thing, that is – whatever happened to the Spoon of Doom?

# Chapter Seventeen

As soon as Uncle Percy's ambulance left the factory, I went back to get it. You see, I realised almost immediately that I had a very small pocket of time to get the spoon and remove it, before someone official appeared at Piddler's demanding an explanation as to what exactly had happened that night.

After all, it's not every day that porridge plants explode into a sea of gruel and grubs. So, while Ernie went to phone Mum, Mandy and me made for the porridge room.

'Don't touch it,' I warned, as we waded through the gunge. 'Percy says that if you touch the spoon it takes you over.'

Mandy frowned. 'But what exactly are we going to do with it?'

I wasn't sure.

'Put it back where my dad hid it?' I suggested.

That seemed the sensible solution.

'Can't,' said Mandy. 'The picture frame's ruined. And, anyway, what if your dad does decide to sell Piddler's – Snoodle will get his hands on it.'

I clambered onto the gantry and peered at the thing (still lying spoon-like where Percy had thrown it).

'So what should I do with it?'

'Hide it until we can think of something better.'

That didn't sound much of a solution. And anyway, where do you hide a wooden spoon?

'With other wooden spoons of course,' said Mandy, as if I was silly for not knowing. 'Stick it in your kitchen utensils pot.'

'My what?'

'The place you stick your spatulas and slatted spoons,' said Mandy, raising her eyebrow.

She'd obviously never been to tea at the Grub house. We don't have spatulas and slotted spoons. But Mum did have one single wooden spoon that she used for baking.

'I can't put it next to that,' I said. 'What if Mum used it by mistake? She'd be cursed for ever. And our town would be smothered to death by her rock cakes. Trust me, that would be even worse than porridge.'

Mandy shrugged. 'Well, stick it in a box of knick-knacks somewhere. Haven't you got a loft? Or an understairs cupboard, or something? Put it in the box with your Christmas decorations, or inside an old suitcase, that sort of thing.'

It didn't sound very scientific.

'Maybe I could sell it to a museum?' I said. 'We could do with the cash.'

Mandy shook her head. 'Someone will steal it, Albert.'

And somehow I knew she was right.

'Some things are better lost for ever,' she said wisely.

For someone so pink, Mandy can certainly make you stop and think.

So I did as she suggested. I wrapped it in my coat, and took it home. Then I packed it up along with that smelly old book that Ernie had given me, and a brief account of my own experiences of the spoon (just in case I got hit by a bus and someone needed to know how dangerous the thing really was), and stuck the lot inside an old box of knick-knacks in our loft.

Dad never asked me what I'd done with it. And I'm glad he didn't. (I don't think he'd sleep quite so soundly at night if he knew that evil spoon was sitting just a metre above his head.) It was enough for him that it was no longer in Piddler's.

And there the story should have ended. Pretty happily ever after. Except I'd forgotten about the annual bug-botherers car-boot sale. My parents do it every year. They choose some poor unfortunate creepy crawly somewhere in the world, and raise money to protect its home. Lovely.

Not really.

Because while I was up at Piddler's having my daily after-school porridge-pounding lessons from Ernie (I can proudly report that my forearms have now grown by two centimetres since I started two months ago), Mum and Dad had a clear out. They emptied the entire attic and carted everything off to the car-boot sale. The spoon and the book were gone. And I've no idea who bought them. What I do know is that Uncle Percy was at the sale. Dad had wheeled him there for an outing. And Smedley Snoodle also put in an appearance. (He and Dad are now firm friends – though I'm sure it's just worm love.) But whether or not they bought the spoon, I can't say.

All I can do is watch and wait. And scan the newspapers. Because, sooner or later I know someone somewhere will come a cropper at the hands of the Spoon of Doom. I just hope it's not you.

Also by Sam Hay…

*"It was the eve of my eleventh birthday and life was about to go down the pan. Completely!"*

Billy doesn't want to Dream the Dream and spend the rest of his life as a plumber. He wants to be a professional footballer. So imagine his surprise when he wakes up to find a hoodie-angel in his room. And when he learns that he has been given a mission – to protect Thelma Potts, the meanest girl in the school, from danger…